Being the new girl in school is never fun.

I'm used to it, though. Spotting potential new friends, identifying the cliques to avoid, figuring out the school's layout... Been there, done that.

Being accused of murder before the first class even starts? That's new.

R.W. WALLACE

Author of the Ghost Detective Series

FIRST IMPRESSIONS

A Young Adult Mystery Short Story

First Impressions
by R.W. Wallace

Copyright © 2019 by R.W. Wallace

Copy editing by Jinxie Gervasio
Cover by the author
Cover Illustration 85978840 © Sandra Matics | 123rf.com
Cover Illustration 36076509 © Sakorn Singsuwan | 123rf.com

All characters and events in this book, other than those clearly in the public domain, are fictitious and any resemblance to real persons, living or dead, is purely coincidental.

All rights reserved. No part of this publication may be reproduced, distributed, or transmitted in any form or by any means, including photocopying, recording, or other electronic or mechanical methods, without the prior written permission of the publisher, except in the case of brief quotations embodied in critical reviews and certain other noncommercial uses permitted by copyright law. For permission requests, write to the publisher, addressed "Attention: Permissions Coordinator," at the address below.

www.rwwallace.com

ISBN: [979-10-95707-11-0]

Main category—Fiction
Other category—Mystery

First Edition

14 13 12 11 10 / 10 9 8 7 6 5 4 3 2 1

Also by R.W. Wallace

Mystery

The Tolosa Mystery Series
The Red Brick Haze (free)
The Red Brick Cellars

Ghost Detective Shorts (coming soon)
Just Desserts
Lost Friends
Family Bonds
Till Death
Common Ground

Short Stories
Hidden Horrors
Critters
Gertrude and the Trojan Horse
First Impressions
Let Them Eat Cake
Out of Sight
Two's Company

Science Fiction (short stories)
The Vanguard
Quarantine (Lollapalooza)
Common Enemies (Lollapalooza)

Adventure (short stories)
Size Matters

Fantasy (short stories)
Unexpected Consequences
Morbier Impossible

FIRST IMPRESSIONS

Everybody knows it's no fun to be the new kid in school. It's important to get off to a good start, make a good first impression.

My first day as a senior in my new school? I got accused of murder.

So much for first impressions.

ೞ

I prepared for this day for *weeks*.

I studied the maps, both of the town and the school. How long would it take me to walk to school? Ten minutes. Was there a bus I could take if it rained? No, better get a decent raincoat and an umbrella. Where was the nearest supermarket, gas station, or anything else that could keep me supplied in sugar in case of emergency? There was a tiny supermarket not even a hundred meters from the school, and a gas station a little further out for when the supermarket was closed.

The school itself seemed boringly predictable (total fail in the research department on this point, the school was anything but). The yard was a square, surrounded by awnings on all sides. Two buildings stood two stories tall, one on the east side of the yard, the other on the west. It was one of those constructs from the seventies, one huge, beige brick, with hundreds of identical windows, managing to look like a prison even without the bars (actually, now that I think of it, there *were* bars—on the ground floor windows). To the north, the school was shut off from the rest of the world by a ten-meter-high wall (adding to the prison feels), and to the south, a simple fence with a gate that was guarded by a lady who seemed like she'd been seated there since the seventies.

Three days before school started, my mom took me shopping. It's an activity I usually loathe, but I needed to look presentable (but preferably with ripped holes in the right places), cool (but not too cool, I'm a nice girl and a bit of a nerd at heart), and approachable (because there was no way *I*'d be the one to approach the others).

Less than two hours, a few euros (in my mom's case) and several tears (in my case) later, I arrived home ready to start a new and better life.

Little did I know that having the right rips in my jeans would soon be the least of my worries.

ಚಿ

THE SCHOOL OPENED its doors (well, the door in the fence, not the doors to the buildings, as I was soon to discover) at eight. Classes started at eight thirty.

Being a good girl, and terrified of being late, I went through the gate at two past eight.

You'd expect the school yard to be empty at that ungodly hour, but no. Seemed like my future classmates (whichever ones they were—this school had five hundred students and only twenty-five of them were in my class) were eager to come back to school—or at the very least, to meet up with their friends that they hadn't seen in over two months.

I sidled along the west building, keeping to the shadows offered by the awning, while trying to keep an eye on everyone in the schoolyard.

My first mistake.

Since I was so focused on every single movement I could see in the center of the yard, I didn't look at where I was putting my feet. So when I stepped straight onto some poor soul's ankle, I didn't even have the reflex to not put all my weight down, or side-step, or *something*. Anything. No, I just continued walking, putting all my weight on my foot before tripping a little because, well, someone's ankle isn't all that stable.

I heard a loud yelp, followed by an *oof*—as I landed ass-first in the lap of my poor target.

Broke my fall quite nicely, so I bounced right back up.

Him, not so much.

"I'm so sorry!" I yelled, putting my hands on my cheeks, then reaching toward his ankle (as if that would do any good at this point), back to my face, toward his stomach (where he probably had an ass-shaped imprint).

I ended up shoving my hands in my pockets.

"I'm so sorry," I repeated. "I didn't see you there."

The poor guy curled into a fetal position, with one hand on his stomach and the other on his ankle. I hadn't gotten a good look at his face, but he seemed tall (then again, everyone's tall compared to me) and had short, curly hair. His skin a smooth brown a couple of shades darker than what I could obtain by spending three months in the sun. Jeans ripped at the knees, and his t-shirt a plain white affair that might have hugged his muscles if he'd had any to write home about.

"How is that even possible?" he wheezed.

"Should've paid attention, man," a voice called from behind me. "She was walking like a blind woman."

I turned to look at the voice's origin and was surprised to discover that the entire wall was occupied by guys, propped up against the dirty wall, their long legs spread out in front of them.

How had I walked past all of them and not noticed a single one? How had I avoided stepping on *them*?

The guy who spoke must have read the question on my face. "We all pulled our legs out of the way," he explained. "Gotta watch where you're going, man."

I briefly considered informing him I wasn't a man, but quickly figured it wasn't worth the effort.

I bent down and patted the air above the wounded guy's head, saying, "I'm really, really sorry. Won't happen again, I promise." Then I took off.

Well, that was one guy that wouldn't be asking me out anytime soon.

At the far end of the building, I found an unoccupied section of wall and decided this was my spot. This was where I would observe the cliques of this school and figure out which one I wanted to be a part of.

Managing to actually integrate said group would be step two, and I'd worry about that once step one was completed.

I quickly concluded that the group of blonde girls standing only a few meters away were not my type. For one, I don't have blonde hair, and that seemed to be a requirement. In fact, three of the girls were nagging the fourth one because she'd let her roots grow out over the summer. No amount of arguing that she'd done it on purpose and that it was the latest thing in Paris could persuade the trio. In less than five minutes, the tune of the fourth one changed to, "I just haven't had the time, but I'll get it done tonight."

I inwardly rolled my eyes. These were the cool girls, I just knew it. They're the same everywhere (okay, they don't all have blonde hair, but you get my drift) and anyone's best policy should be to stay as far away as possible. Even the girls *inside* these groups aren't safe. They're like cannibals, frequently eating their own, to make sure everybody stays on their toes, and to confirm the position of whoever the leader is.

I'm pretty sure girls like these are the actual reason other girls never go alone to the bathroom. Everybody makes fun of girls always going in pairs, but they don't realize it's a survival thing. You do *not* want to find yourself alone in a room with the four Blondies.

And now I needed to use the toilet.

I checked my watch. It was only ten past eight.

I looked around, searching for a door with a woman on it. Or even a man. I'm not that picky when I'm desperate.

Since I was increasingly convinced that I wouldn't be able to find a bathroom until the school officially opened in twenty minutes, I was getting desperate real fast.

There had to be some place we could use the restroom while we were out during recess, right?

I pushed my way past the Blondie group and approached a short red-head. I had yet to see a red-head as the leader in a school, so I figured she was a safe bet.

"Excuse me," I said, flashing her my best smile. "You wouldn't happen to know where the restrooms are? I'm new in this school."

The girl looked at me with slightly unfocused brown eyes and for a moment I worried she was a foreign exchange student who didn't speak the language.

She squinted down at me, then her eyebrows shot up. "Oh, sorry, I thought you were Léna." She pointed to the other building, at the northernmost corner. "The toilets are over there."

"Thank you." Hefting my backpack higher on my back, I almost sprinted across the yard, all the while searching with my eyes for one of those wonderful signs.

I found it exactly where the girl told me I would, but a group of at least fifteen girls were blocking my way.

"Excuse me," I tried as I pushed my way into the throng. "I need to use the restroom, please."

"Door's locked," a dark-eyed beauty told me when I tried to get past her.

I was getting really desperate, and even though I realized she was probably right, I needed to check for myself.

Needless to say, that group of girls would not be my friends, either. Stabbing someone with your elbow as you try to get past them, or stepping on someone's sandaled feet, are not the best first impressions if you want to make friends.

To make matters worse, the door was indeed locked.

I checked my watch again. Eight thirteen.

I wasn't going to make it.

So like I always do in stressful situations, I improvised.

And no, this is never a good idea, but I never learn.

I noticed there was a very narrow space between the building and the huge north wall cutting us off from the rest of the world. When I went to check, I saw that there were windows, most certainly leading to the bathrooms. It was one of those wide openings that are almost at the ceiling—so you get light in, but nobody can stand outside and perv on the people taking care of business on the inside.

I jumped up to look—the window was cracked open.

Okay, that did it. I was going in.

I abandoned my backpack in the corner, wrongfully thinking I'd be back to get it in a minute or two. Then I took aim, crouched down, and jumped.

Not at the window, mind. It was just too high. I jumped at the wall. Then used that as a jumping board to bound back at the school building.

I knocked my forehead into concrete, but I managed to grab hold of the windowsill and pull myself up.

Using an elbow to force the window open, I poured myself through the opening, and jumped into the bathroom feet first.

Victory!

A quick glance told me there was no way I was going out the way I came in because it was higher up the wall in here, and I had nothing to use for purchase. Right then I didn't care.

I just wanted to pee.

Which was to become my main line of defense.

I ran to the closest stall, slammed open the door, and started opening my jeans before I was even inside. It wasn't like anybody else was going to come in there, right?

As I could *finally* let free, my teeth had goosebumps and I uttered a shivering moan.

At which point, a voice said, "What on Earth is going on in here? Do *not* tell me someone's started in on the depravities *before* the school year has even started."

That was definitely an adult.

And that ray of light coming in from the left? Yup, probably from the open door.

Never one to abort any action once I've started, I stayed seated.

A woman stepped in front of my open stall. She was tall, blonde, carrying an extra kilo or two around the midsection, and dressed like a hippie. Long flowery skirt, loose white blouse. I guessed her hair was naturally straight because the lack of free curls definitely looked odd.

"*What* is going on here?" Only teachers could put that much accusation into a simple question.

"What does it look like?" I replied. I was finally done but didn't want to get up in front of the teacher, so I stayed seated.

Her eyes scanned the room as she gesticulated with her skinny arms. "It looks like—" She drew in a quick breath.

Screamed.

Some sort of survival instinct kicked in for me, and I slammed both arms outward, holding on to the walls of my stall. Maybe I was expecting them to fall down on me?

I did *not* think of getting dressed.

So naturally, when the group of girls from earlier swarmed the restroom, I was still sitting on the toilet with my jeans around my ankles.

When the titters started, I decided it was time to cut my losses. Jumped up and pulled at my jeans at lightning speed. Of course, the panties didn't quite follow, so they sat halfway down my ass, making it feel like I was still naked.

The teacher was still screaming.

"Hey," the pretty girl from earlier said as she looked into the stall next to mine. "Who killed Madame Couteloup?"

൙

So there I was, sitting in the headmaster's office with two police officers staring at me from across the headmaster's desk. The man himself was leaning against the window (with bars, since we were on the ground floor), but hadn't said a word since I walked through the door. Next to him stood the hippie teacher from earlier, who *finally* stopped screaming the minute she saw the uniforms.

I wondered if I got two female officers because they believed I was most likely to confess to women, or if there really were a lot of women in the police force today. I considered looking into it as a potential career.

"Did you kill Madame Couteloup?" the youngest of the two asked me. She had silky black hair and makeup so subtle you couldn't even tell it was there unless you looked for it. I was thinking being a cop couldn't be that bad if she could look this good on the job. Then the question sank in.

Maybe make sure I wasn't convicted of murder before deciding to become a cop.

"Of course I didn't!" I said. Maybe I should call my lawyer. Or my mom. That's what they always did in the American series on TV. Called their lawyers, that is. I wasn't even sure that was how it worked in France.

Should've watched more French sitcoms.

Do French police procedurals even exist? There was so much crap on TV, I seriously considered giving up on it altogether until my parents got Netflix. Since then I'd become *slightly* addicted.

"Mademoiselle Gérard," the old police officer said (she must have been at least forty, possibly even older given the number of gray hairs I spotted). "You were discovered on the scene of the crime, not having raised the alarm yourself, and with your pants down."

I frowned at her. "You make me sound like a sexual offender. You don't get caught with your pants down in a murder case." What *do* you get caught with? A smoking gun?

"And yet," the old one said, "you were."

"I needed to pee!" I explained. "The door was locked, so I went through the window. I never looked inside the stall where Madame what's-her-name was found. If I had, I assure you, I would have raised the alarm."

Possibly after relieving myself, but I didn't say that out loud.

The old one narrowed her eyes slightly and bent her head to write something in a black notebook I hadn't noticed until now.

I craned my neck trying to see what she was writing, but the angle was all wrong.

"What makes you say the door was locked?"

"I…I checked the door," I said. "It didn't open. And the other girls told me it was closed."

The old one continued taking notes while the young one talked. "Which girls?"

"Uh…" I looked to the headmaster for help, but he stood there like a statue, making me wonder if he was even awake. "I'm new in this school," I explained. "I don't know anybody."

"So a girl you don't know tells you the door's locked and you automatically believe her?"

"Why would she lie?" I caught myself before answering that question myself. "And I checked. It was locked."

"Actually," the young one said, "It wasn't. The hinges are a little rusty, so you have to push quite hard for it to open."

I was floored. Though not really surprised. It's always the same, isn't it? Step on others to get higher. Take no prisoners.

Those girls had taken one look at me and decided it was more fun to tell me the bathroom was closed than to let me through and explain how to get the door open.

"I didn't know that," I said, my voice small and uneven. I decided I didn't need to look the officers in the eyes and studied the edge of the headmaster's desk instead.

It was made of wood.

That was all I got.

"We asked the other students about you," one of the officers said. I couldn't tell them apart just from their voices. "Seems like you have a tendency toward violence."

"What?" My gaze snapped up. "Nobody here even knows my name!"

"And yet you've managed to assault several of them already."

I stared at the two women in incomprehension. I turned to the headmaster and the hippie teacher, but they were no better. Serious expressions all around, and accusation obvious in their eyes.

Four adults in the room, and they all believed I killed some teacher I'd never even met!

"One boy," the young one said, "claims you stepped and sat on him while he was listening to music, minding his own business."

"I didn't see—," I started, but nobody was listening.

"Another girl claims you pretended to be her friend Léna in order to extract information from her."

"I asked her where the bathroom—"

"Five different girls claim you attacked them with your elbows and stepped on their toes as you, for some reason, had to go *through* their group."

"I had to *pee*, and they were blocking the door to the bathroom!"

I finally got to finish a sentence, but my yelling was followed by a resounding silence.

The old one filled an entire little page with notes, and as she turned the page, she asked, "How well did you know Madame Couteloup?"

"I didn't." I drew a deep breath and let it out slowly. "I want to call my mom."

The headmaster spoke up for the first time, making me jump in my chair. "She's already been notified of the situation. She's on her way."

That didn't sound as reassuring as it should.

The young one folded her hands and cocked her head as she narrowed her eyes at me. "What did Madame Couteloup do to deserve your wrath, young lady?"

"I didn't even know her! The only time I ever saw her she was already dead."

Nobody believed me, of course. And although I didn't know the dead teacher before, during the upcoming interrogation, I started to get a pretty good picture.

The old one: "Did she put you in a class with people you didn't like?"

"I wouldn't know. I don't know which class I'm in yet, and I don't know anybody in this school."

The new one: "Did you make sexual advances on her and she turned you down?"

What?

The old one: "Did *she* make advances on *you*?"

Ew.

The headmaster (I must not be the only one thinking this interrogation was going off the rails): "Did she accuse you of something you didn't do? Didn't give you a chance to explain? Went straight for the punishments?"

With the theme of the previous questions, a frisson ran through me at the mention of punishments, but I was going to assume he was talking about detention or extra homework. I shook my head.

The hippie teacher: "Did she give you a lecture on how the world would go under if we all wanted to eat ecological food? Did she tell you that you were egoistical and judgmental?"

I shook my head.

The headmaster: "Maybe she refused your request to use the bathroom, claiming it wouldn't open until eight thirty, only to use the premises herself?"

I was less and less offended by their questions, and more and more convinced the dead woman was one of those teachers you avoid at all costs. The kind adults talk about thirty years later to illustrate how awful school was back in their time.

The police officers seemed happy to let the teacher and headmaster do the interrogation. In fact, the old one was still taking notes, and the young one had shifted in her chair so she had both me and the school employees in her sight.

The hippie teacher: "Did she steal your snack, claiming she did you a service since it didn't have an ecological label?"

The hippie teacher: "Did she brag about her vacation on Isle de Ré, going on and on about the hunks who supposedly flirted with her on the beach?"

The surreal direction this interrogation was going in made my fear and stress fall away. I forgot I was accused of murder.

"I've been to Isle de Ré," I told her. "If you like some calm when you go to the beach, it's not ideal, honestly. And the people are…fake."

"Exactly!" the hippie teacher exclaimed, waving her arms. "It's for fake people who have no real friends and just want to show off their tan and their money."

I nodded. "Then why do you care that she taunts you about it? If it's not actually something you want?"

I might have been the youngest person in the room, but I felt like I just might have been the only one with the right life experience to get through to this woman. I'd changed schools so many times over the past ten years, I'd literally stopped counting. My dad could never keep a job for more than a year (his record being a month and a half) and every time he changed jobs, we had to change cities.

I didn't know what it was that he did which made a move a necessity, and I didn't want to know.

What I did know was that the new girl was rarely welcomed with open arms.

I'd decided it was mostly due to fear and jealousy. Fear that I might take their place, or somehow modify the power structure that was already in place. Jealousy because I was awesome.

Yes, that was what I was going with. Deal with it.

If you looked at it that way, the verbal aggressions from fellow students weren't that bad. They criticized my clothes? Probably meant they were dope. They claimed I wasn't cool enough? It was obvious to them that I was capable of taking their place if I wanted. They purposely didn't invite me to parties when the entire school was going? Their loss. I'd just hang out with my real friends.

Because no matter which school, no matter which city, every school had nice people. You just needed to find them.

"I'm sure there are other teachers in this school," I told the hippie teacher. "People who are nice. The mean ones are just noise, you know."

"That's easy for you to say!" the teacher said, her eyes going a little too wide for comfort. "You haven't suffered the woman for ten long years."

I pitied the woman, I really did.

School can be a mean place. But the thing that saves us is that it's not forever. Junior high is just four years. High school just three. Now, a year can seem interminable when you're suffering, but if you do manage to put things into perspective, it's possible to just hunker down and power through.

But this woman, the hippie teacher, was stuck here. She'd chosen school as her place of work, and so had her bully.

"She was really that mean, huh?" I wanted to go over and give the woman a hug, but something told me to stay put.

I was vaguely aware of the three other people in the room—I heard the headmaster's raspy breath and the old one's pencil scratching across the notepad—but all my focus was on the bully victim.

"What did she do this time?" I asked.

The teacher's breath came in irregular gasps and a single tear streaked down her cheek. Her hands curled into fists at her sides. "She had a picture," she said, her voice wobbly.

"A picture of what?" Not that I really needed to know, I saw where this was going.

"Of me working in my back yard. She must have been visiting with one of my neighbors." Her eyes were distant, probably looking back to the time it happened. "It was really hot and humid, and I had a thousand weeds to get rid of. So I decided to work wearing just an old bikini.

"In the picture, you can see the top of my ass, the cellulite on my thighs, and my stomach bunching into a…huge, fat blob." She met my eyes, imploring me to understand. "She was going to leave them around school, so all the kids would find them."

Being bullied by a fellow teacher was one thing. If she also had to suffer the taunts of her students, probably for years to come, I could understand her desperation. Even I might have found that to be too much.

Kids can be *mean*.

"Killing her wasn't the right solution, though," I told her.

She hung her head, her straight hair falling forward to cover her face. "I know," she whispered. "But she had the pictures in her purse, ready to distribute, and I *panicked*."

Holding my breath, I turned to meet the old lady police officer's eyes. Did that really just happen?

She nodded at me and mouthed, *good job*.

There was some relief at no longer being suspected of murder, but mostly I felt sad. A woman who'd been bullied for years finally had enough and wanted to stand up for herself, only to end up even worse off.

The headmaster straightened. "I believe you may return to class," he said.

Nodding, I stood up. I took a step toward the door, then changed my mind.

I ran to the hippie teacher and embraced her in a hug.

☙

"Come sit over here." The pretty girl from in front of the bathroom that morning waved me over to her seat by the window as I made my way toward the back of the class. "Saved you a spot."

Word had spread about one teacher offing the other, and rumor had it I knew all the juicy details. The Blondies tried to befriend me over lunch (it seemed like they'd even be ready to forego the hair color rule for me), and now this group.

"Thanks," I said, "but I've always preferred the dark side of the room." I point in that direction, only to be met with a pair of dark, sparkly eyes.

Pretty.

Why was he looking at me like that?

I slowly made my way toward him—couldn't really go anywhere else after what I said to the pretty girl—trying to figure out if I was supposed to know him from somewhere.

"There's a free spot here," he said, waving to the chair next to him. He had his foot propped up on it, which might explain why the seat was still free. The seats at the back of a classroom were always the first to be filled.

He lowered his foot to the ground, rather gingerly for a seventeen-year-old.

Then I really noticed his clothes. Ripped jeans. White t-shirt. Brown skin and curly black hair.

"You're the guy I stepped on this morning!" I exclaimed. I felt my cheeks growing warm and seriously considered sitting next to the pretty girl.

He flashed a smile at me, and I went a little weak in the knees. Who cares if he didn't fill out his t-shirt. This guy had *charm*.

"You may have to make it up to me," he said. "I wouldn't mind a little help with Maths." He nodded to the blackboard where the maths teacher had yet to make an appearance.

He pulled out the chair for me, never taking his eyes off mine. "And maybe a coffee or an ice cream after school?"

I dropped into the chair, my backpack still on my back. "Sure," I managed to say.

Turns out you *can* remedy a first impression. Who knew?

THANK YOU

THANK YOU FOR reading *First Impressions*. I hope you enjoyed it!

If you liked the story, you might want to check out some of my other books mentioned on the next page. It's mostly mysteries, but a few other genre short stories will pop up, too.

And don't forget that the first book of my *Tolosa Mystery* series, *The Red Brick Haze*, is available for free on my website.

R.W. Wallace
www.rwwallace.com

Also by R.W. Wallace

Mystery

THE TOLOSA MYSTERY SERIES
The Red Brick Haze (free)
The Red Brick Cellars
The Red Brick Basilica

GHOST DETECTIVE SHORTS (COMING SOON)
Just Desserts
Lost Friends
Family Bonds
Till Death
Family History
Common Ground
Heritage
Eternal Bond
New Beginnings

SHORT STORIES
Cold Blue Eternity
Hidden Horrors
Critters
Gertrude and the Trojan Horse
First Impressions
Let Them Eat Cake
Out of Sight
Two's Company
Like Mother Like Daughter

Fantasy (Short Stories)
Unexpected Consequences
Morbier Impossible
A Second Chance

Science Fiction (Short Stories)
The Vanguard

Lollapalooza Shorts
Quarantine
Common Enemies
Coiled Danger
Mars Meeting

Adventure (Short Stories)
Size Matters